In Granny's Garden

In Granny's Garden

Sarah Harrison & Mike Wilks

Jonathan Cape   Thirty Bedford Square   London

First published in Great Britain 1980
Illustrations copyright © 1980 by Mike Wilks
Text copyright © 1980 by Sarah Harrison

Jonathan Cape Ltd, 30 Bedford Square, London WC1

British Library Cataloguing in Publication Data

Harrison, Sarah
In granny's garden.
1. Wilks, Mike
I. Title
823'.9'1J   PZ7.H256/

ISBN 0 224 01867 1

Printed in the United States of America

For Laurence and Fanny,
Their grannies, and their great-grannies
(whose gardens are nothing like this)

In Granny's Garden

My Granny had a garden, jungly wild,
Through which I used to wander as a child;
It was a most exploring kind of place
Where vines and webs would trail across your face
To hold you back.

And in its depths I fancied that there lay
Dragons and dodos, predator and prey.
And in each murky thicket, track, and glade
A half-seen monster grazing in the shade
With downcast eyes.

The gardener had long since left his post
To make way for this prowling, unseen host,
And Granny sat indoors among her palms,
Dreaming of India and reading psalms
And sipping tea.

One humid day amid the hanging green
I saw a tree where no tree should have been:
It rose, all sleek and black, a serpent trunk,
Out of the pool my unicorns had drunk
When conjured up.

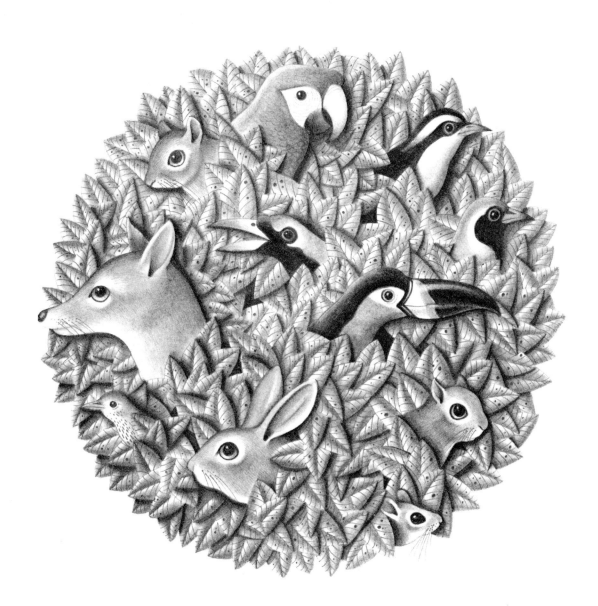

I walked around the pool and wondered long
If that tall, towering tree trunk, smooth and strong,
Had sprouted overnight. It *couldn't* be . . .
Its presence was a mystery to me.
And then—it moved!

It bent all curvily and winding down,
While I stood rooted to the quaking ground,
And through the treetops, down from outer space,
It lowered not its branches, but its face.
A brontosaurus's face.

A brontosaurus, as I'm sitting here,
To my complete amazement did appear,
And bent upon me his enormous eyes,
As bosky and benign as warm night skies,
And blinked at me.

His lashes like bus shelters overhung
His gaze, and from his cavern-mouth his tongue
Unfurled to wipe his crinkly canvas cheeks
As though he boggled at this king of freaks,
This Eton-collared boy.

We stared, with dignity, that beast and I,
With panic well-suppressed and steady eye.
And then, the closer to observe my frame,
He stirred a tidal wave and out he came
Upon the bank.

The oily pool churned up like raging seas
As brontosaurus flexed his scaly knees,
And reared his gentle, treetop-dwarfing figure
To its full height—he was without doubt bigger
Than ever I had thought.

With plodding steps he sploshed the squishy mud,
Sinking boy-deep and chewing oak tree cud.
And then his pillar-legs all round me splayed,
And I, an insect in their massive shade,
Peeped palely out.

He looked about him, wondering where I cowered,
And mighty branches all around us showered
As his huge neck scythed to and fro on high,
Peering and craning, trying to spot the fly,
The fly I seemed to him.

Swoosh! Darkness! As he bent and looked
Between his horny knees so bandy-crook'd
And beamed engagingly, though upside down,
A smile that could have sucked up half a town,
And charmed me out.

I faltered forth and ventured faint: "Hallo."
Whereon he spoke, in bell-like tones and low,
A cultured voice, distinguished and urbane,
Booming from my brontosaurus came
And shook the trees.

"A pleasant spot, though marshy," he averred,
While I could manage not another word;
Civilities completed, he began
To tell me of the world from which he sprang
So long ago.

A world of steaming swamps and teeming seas,
Of far-flung rocks and giant ferns, like trees;
A world where dragons laid their leathery eggs
And lizards raced on earthquake-making legs
Like seven-league boots.

A world where scaly fists and spines and horns
Clashed in gargantuan battles at life's dawn,
And clouds were shaken by wingbeats so vast
It seemed a ghostly armor thundered past,
Blocking the sun . . .

Tyrannosaurus stalked, his grinning jaws
Inviting prey into his deadly claws;
While gentle brontosaurus, the good sport,
Just wallowed in the swamps, a first-rate sort,
It seemed to me.

I listened all agog, I could not go,
Until my brontosaurus stemmed the flow
Of words, and said politely, "Mind if I submerge?
I can't gainsay it when I get the urge,
Immerse I must."

Like Stonehenge on the move he crashed away.
My voice was lost when I begged him to stay.
He suddenly became a tree once more,
Except for bow waves crashing on the shore,
And on my shoes.

I rushed, I fled, back to recount my tale.
I stamped through bushes, brambles, over mud and shale,
And up the steps with deerlike leaps I sped—
A prehistoric world was in my head,
Ready to tell.

"I saw a brontosaurus!" I burst out,
I couldn't keep composed, I had to shout,
"He's in your garden, plain as he can be.
His neck's so big I thought it was a tree,
He *talks* as well!"

Then Granny turned on me her pale, old eyes;
She looked so small and frail, and yet so wise;
And rustling the tissue pages of her psalter,
She murmured vaguely, "Yes, that will be Walter,
He's such a dear, one of a dying race,
But then . . . my garden *is* a magic place."